DRAW-IT-YOURSELF ADVENTURES

ALIEN ATTACK

Little, Brown and Company
Hachette Book Group
1290 Avenue of the Americas, New York, NY 10104
Visit us at lb-kids.com

Originally published in 2016 by Scholastic in Great Britain
First U.S. Edition: May 2017

Little, Brown and Company is a division of Hachette Book Group, Inc.
The Little, Brown name and logo are trademarks of Hachette Book Group, Inc.

The publisher is not responsible for websites (or their content) that are not owned by the publisher.

Book design by Chris Judge

ISBNs: 978-0-316-464215 (hardcover)

Printed in the United States of America

LSC-C

10 9 8 7 6 5 4 3 2 1

DRAW-IT-YOURSELF ADVENTURES

ALIEN ATTACK

ANDREW JUDGE & CHRIS JUDGE

Little, Brown and Company
New York Boston

I know what you are thinking.

You want to flip ahead to the exciting parts.

Like the **ESCAPE FROM THE ALIEN ZOO** on page 95 and the **EPIC SPACE BATTLE** on page 106.

I bet you do!

But first we have to get the boring parts out of the way.

Just kidding! This is a book about **ALIENS**! It's **ALL** exciting.

What's also great about this book is that **YOU** get to join in. So grab a pencil and draw some **CRATERS** on the moon and another **SOLAR PANEL** on the space station! You can also draw some more stars if you want.

You don't need to draw any of the missing pieces on this spaceship though.

It's not unfinished.

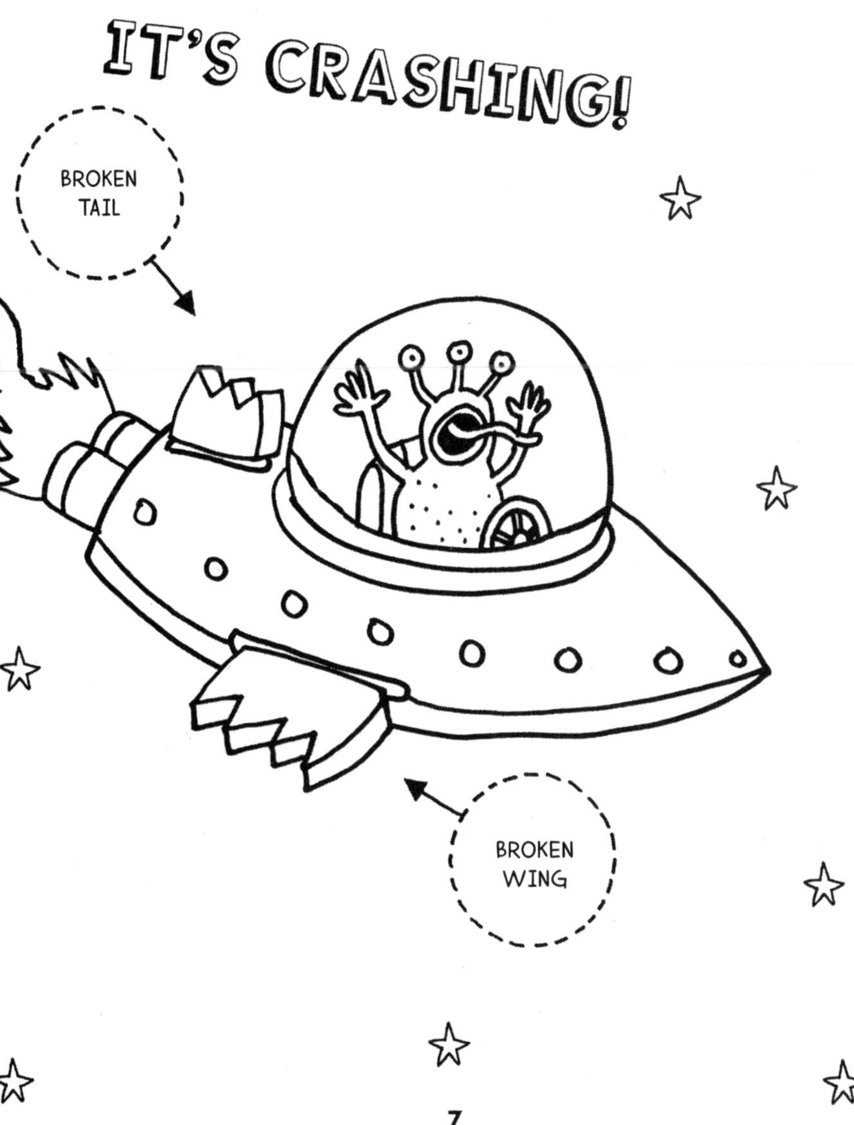

Meet B'ob. He's one of the heroes in this story.
Say hello to the reader, B'ob.

says B'ob.

Okay. So maybe now is a bad time.
We'll come back later.

Now where was I? Ah yes! **DOODLES**. This isn't just a story about aliens. It's also filled with Doodles. What's a Doodle, you ask?*

This is a Doodle. Daisy Doodle to be precise. She is the other hero of the story.

*You didn't ask? Oh. Well, now you know anyway.

Daisy and her friends live in Doodletown. It is a very nice town, as you can see, except for one **SMALL** problem. Everything is half drawn with bits and pieces missing!

*Can you draw my face, please?

The Doodles are going to need YOUR help. So grab a pencil and finish the Doodles on this page.

So, are you ready to start?

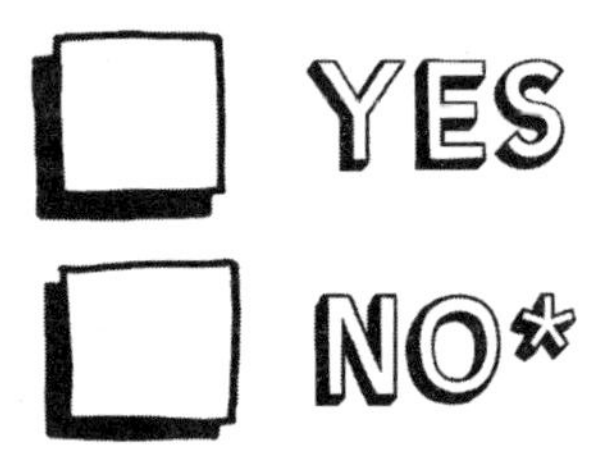

LET'S BEGIN!

*Did you check **NO**? Really? Oh. Turn to page 128.

CHAPTER ONE

SCHOOL!

It is Thursday morning and Daisy Doodle is on her way to school. It is a lovely sunny day. Or maybe it isn't because **THE WEATHER ISN'T DRAWN YET**.

Maybe the sun is shining or maybe there is a **HUGE** thunder and lightning storm. **YOU** decide, because that's the way this book works!

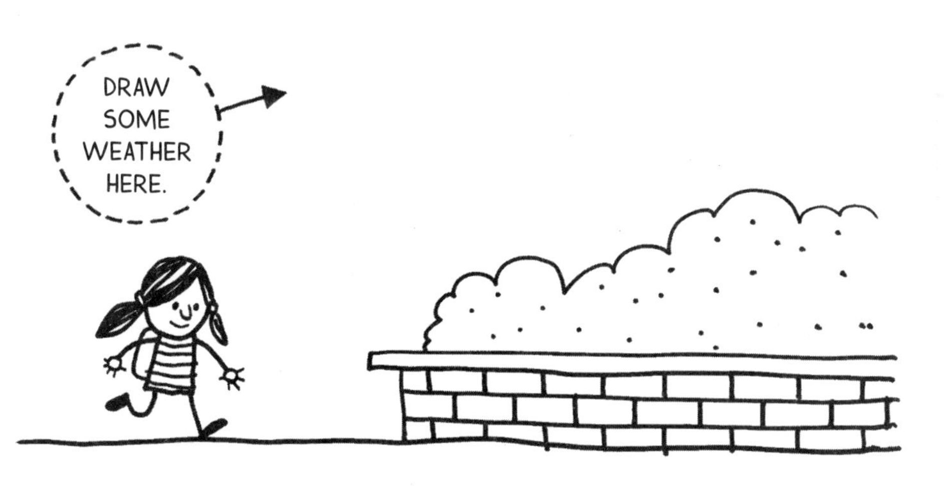

So what's it going to be? Sunshine or rain? Daisy is hoping that it is sunny, because she has forgotten her coat.

Daisy arrives at school in a good mood. Or soaking wet. It really depends on what you drew.

She spots her best friend, Donny, outside the school gates. Donny gives her a big wave and runs over.

"Hey, Daisy. Did you see that movie about the alien invasion last night? It was cool!"

Daisy nods. "Yes, but why do they always make the aliens the bad guys? Some of them must be nice. I bet I could make friends with an alien if it came to visit Doodletown."

Donny laughs. "An alien in Doodletown? That's not going to happen, is it?"

"Well," says Daisy, "if I meet one, I'll let you know."

Daisy and Donny wander over to the playground. The bell hasn't rung yet so everyone is trying to have fun before school starts. Except they have forgotten to bring things to play with.

Look at these guys trying to jump without a jump rope. Can you draw one for them?

And these kids are playing soccer without a ball! Add one in with your pencil.

The bell rings, **DING-A-LING-A-LING!** It is time to line up for class. Miss Scribble comes out of the school to gather everyone together. But she seems to have forgotten something!

She waves her arms in front of her and stumbles around the playground. "Hello? Where is everybody?"

"It looks like she's lost her glasses again," says Daisy.

Can you draw some on her?

"Draw a **BIG MUSTACHE**, too!" says Donny.

Suddenly Miss Scribble can see.

"Ah, there you are," she says, twirling her mustache. **TWIRLING HER MUSTACHE!? WHAT THE—?**

"**EEEEK!** Who drew this mustache on me?" she yells.

The whole class bursts out laughing. It's not every day you see your teacher with a big handlebar mustache.

"That's enough fun for now," says Miss Scribble as she erases her mustache and straightens her glasses. "Everybody line up, please."

The whole class forms a line while Miss Scribble counts them. "Twenty-one, twenty-two. Twenty-two? We are one short. Where is Undrawn John?"

"I'm here," says a voice. "I'm just not drawn yet."

Miss Scribble sighs. "Can somebody please draw Undrawn John?"

Could you please help?

"Follow me," says Miss Scribble as she leads the class to the school entrance.

But look! Someone has erased the door while Miss Scribble wasn't looking.

"This is **RIDICULOUS**!" says Miss Scribble. "The door is gone again! Can anybody help?"

Quick! You had better draw a door before Daisy and her class get into more trouble.

Finally the school yard is empty. Which is too bad because the very next moment something **UNBELIEVABLE** happens.

AN ALIEN SPACESHIP FALLS FROM THE SKY!

Imagine! The one thing Daisy wanted to see and she just missed it by **ONE PAGE**!

The spaceship shoots across the sky, billowing smoke from its tail. Or at least it will be billowing smoke when you draw some billowing smoke.

Exciting stuff, eh?

Meanwhile, inside, Miss Scribble is droning on about space and planets and stars. That might sound a bit **INTERESTING** to you, but Miss Scribble has a way of making the most **EXCITING** thing in the universe sound boring. Do you know any teachers like that?

No? Well, you are one of the lucky ones, I guess.

Miss Scribble is explaining that some planets are made out of rocks and some are made out of gas.

See what I mean? **EXCITING**. Not.

"Our Planet Scratchpad is just the right distance from the sun," she continues. "It is not too hot and not too cold. It is just the right temperature to allow us to live here. Like Goldilocks's porridge. Except it's not porridge. It's a planet. I hope you are taking notes."

Daisy is one of the few students still awake. "What sort of planets do aliens come from, Miss Scribble?"

Miss Scribble pauses mid-drone. "Daisy Doodle, how many times do I have to tell you? Aliens DON'T exist! Stop asking silly questions."

"Okay," says Daisy. "But what is that looking in the window then?"

Miss Scribble **SCREAMS!**

Because there is an **ALIEN** looking in the window!

PLANET
CRATCHPAD
DRAW AN
ALIEN HERE.

CHAPTER TWO

CHASE!

Everybody stares at the window. The alien stares back. "**EEEEK!**" says Miss Scribble helpfully.

The whole class leaps to their feet, knocking over chairs and desks, and races outside. Daisy and Penny are the fastest but even they are not quick enough to catch the alien. There is no sign of it in the yard.

Daisy's heart sinks. "We missed it!"

Penny says, "Look! A clue!" There on the ground are some strangely shaped muddy footprints.

Daisy's eyes widen. "Whoa! It **WAS** an alien!"

The footprints lead from the classroom window out across the school yard.

There are three places the alien could have gone. It's up to you to decide. Where do the footprints lead?

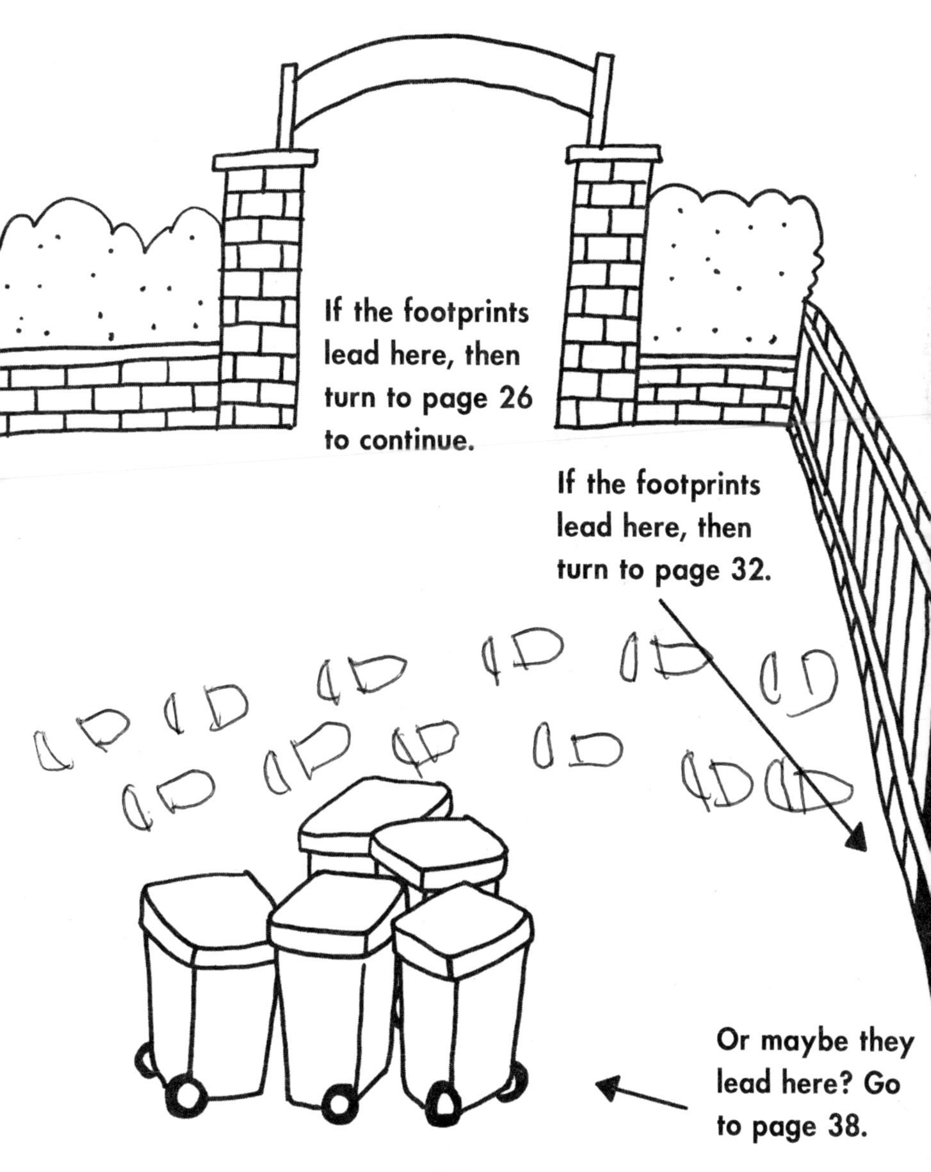

HOLD IT!

Where do you think you are going? You can't just wander out of school without permission. That's **CRAZY**!

You had better go get a permission slip.

Fold down the corner of the page so that you will remember where you are and then go to the principal's office on page 127.

TICK! TICK! TICK!

Good. You're back.
Did you get the permission slip?

Then turn the page and continue.

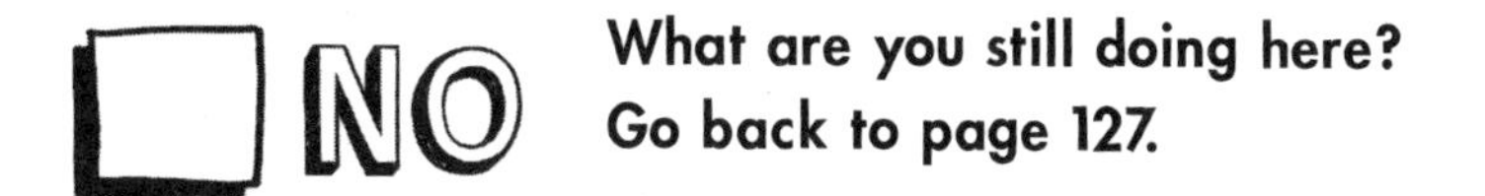

What are you still doing here?
Go back to page 127.

Daisy follows the footprints across the playground and out onto Inky Avenue. It is a busy street—the **PERFECT PLACE** to hide an alien.

It could be peeping over the fence. Or hiding in the doorway. What's that in the mailbox? Could it be on the roof?

Decide where the alien is hiding and draw it in. Daisy **MIGHT** spot it with your help.

Daisy reaches the Doodletown fire station and has a **GREAT IDEA**.

"If I could get up high," she says, looking upward at the tower, "I would be able to spot the alien."

Can you think of a way for her to get up the tower? Draw something to help her.

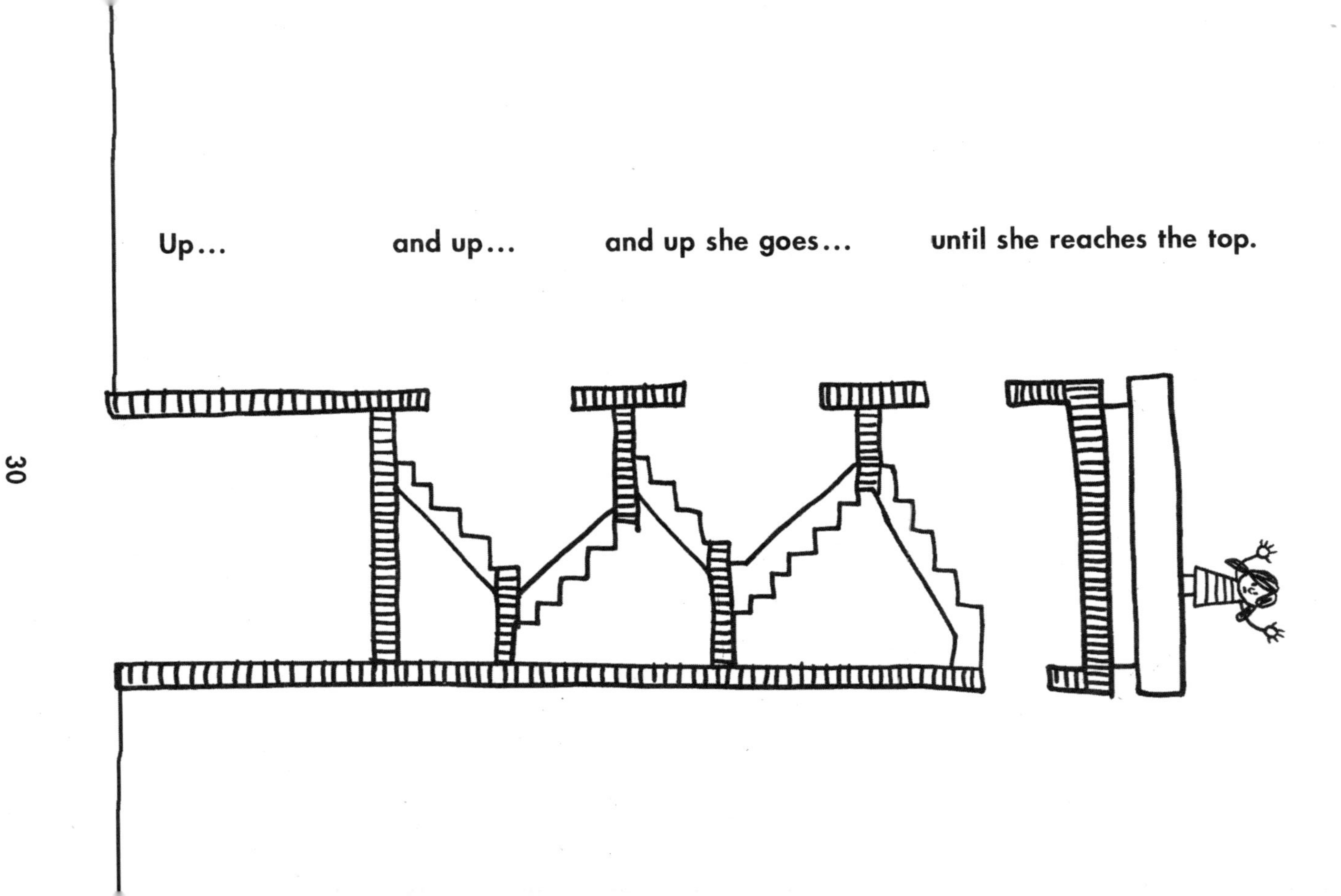
Up...
and up...
and up she goes...
until she reaches the top.

"Phew! Made it!" she says as she stops to catch her breath. Then, "Wow," as she turns around and sees the view spread out below her. She can see **ALL** of Doodletown from here. But no alien. Out at the edge of the town she notices something unusual: a large crater that was not there last Tuesday!

"Now **THAT** is interesting," says Daisy. "I think I will go and take a look."

Turn to page 42.

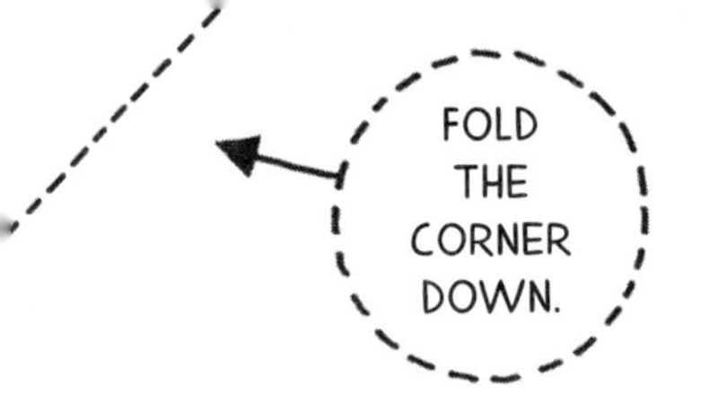

Daisy runs to the gap in the fence and is about to slip through when Chalky the caretaker spots her.

"Where do you think you are going?" asks Chalky.

Daisy points frantically to the gap in the fence. "I'm chasing an alien who went this way."

"Well," says Chalky, "you need permission from the principal to chase aliens outside school grounds."

Daisy rolls her eyes.

You had better do what he says. Fold down the corner of the page so that you will remember where you are and then go to the principal's office on page 127.

Did you get the permission slip on page 127?

No? Well you had better go get it then.
Yes? Great. Let's continue.

Daisy slips through the gap in the fence and into the woods beside the school. She stands still and listens carefully. She realizes she has never noticed all the little noises before.

A bird calls from high up in a tree. A dog barks in the distance. There is a crack of twigs from inside a bush. Something goes "**GORP!**" The wind rustles the leaves.

Excuse me? Did you say "**GORP**"?

Do you know **ANYTHING** that goes "**GORP**"? I don't. It must be the alien!

Daisy takes off running as quick as she can. She races through the woods, ducking under branches and jumping over logs.

Daisy reaches the river, but she has no way across. She is **STUCK**.

What is she going to do?

Maybe you can draw something to help her.

What about a **ROPE SWING**? Or a **FALLEN TREE**? I bet you can think of something good.

Once she is safely across the river, Daisy heads deeper and deeper into the woods. It gets darker and darker as the trees get taller and taller. Soon she is lost.

At last she comes to a clearing.

I need to climb a **REALLY** tall tree to see where I am, thinks Daisy.

Can you help? Draw a **REALLY** tall tree for her to climb.

Daisy climbs the tree and pops her head above the canopy. She looks around to get her bearings.

She spots **SOMETHING STRANGE**. At the edge of the woods, there is a giant crater. That's not **NORMAL**, is it?

"It looks like something has crashed," says Daisy, "and I'm going to find out what!"

Turn to page 42 to find out what is going on.

Daisy races to the recycling bins to catch the alien. She arrives **JUST IN TIME** to see the bins being loaded onto a recycling truck. She looks around desperately for the alien, but there is no sign of it.

From the corner of her eye, she spots something.

"Oh my goodness! Is that the alien in the back of the truck?"

It is! It's the alien peeping out!

Daisy runs toward the alien. But the recycling man **BLOCKS** her way.

"What are you doing here?" he says. "It's dangerous to run behind a truck."

Daisy points to the back of the truck. "But there is an alien in there."

"Is that a fact?" says the man. "Well, your alien might have permission to be here, but **YOU** don't."

FOLD THE CORNER OF THE PAGE.

DRAW THE ALIEN HERE.

He's right. Daisy needs **PERMISSION** to leave the school grounds. Fold down the corner of the page so that you will remember where you are and then go to the principal's office on page 127.

Did you get the permission slip on page 127?

No? Back to page 127 then.
Yes? Okay. Let's keep going.

By the time Daisy gets back from the principal's office with the permission slip, the truck is **GONE**. She has no way of catching up.

Or does she?

"I need a bike or a scooter to catch the truck," she says.

Great idea! Can you draw her something to ride?

Daisy races after the truck. She pedals (or scoots) as fast as she can, but it is **IMPOSSIBLE** to catch. She realizes that the recycling truck is heading to the Doodletown Recycling Center.

But when she gets to the center there is still **NO SIGN** of the truck. There is a **HUGE** pile of cardboard boxes, though. She scrambles up the heap until she reaches the very top. She catches her breath and looks around.

There, in the distance, she spots something **MYSTERIOUS** and **CRATER-ISH**.

"That looks like a **MYSTERIOUS CRATER**!" she says. "I think I will check it out!"

What will happen next? Turn to page 42 to find out!

CHAPTER THREE

SPACESHIP!

Daisy arrives at the crater. She peers over the edge and sees a **CRASHED SPACESHIP**!

AWESOME!

The spaceship, I mean. Not the crashed part. That's not awesome. That's bad.

This must be how the alien got here! Maybe it is nearby.

Daisy creeps closer. The spaceship looks like it is badly damaged. There is a big gash along the side where it had been ripped open in the crash.

You need to rip the page along the line.

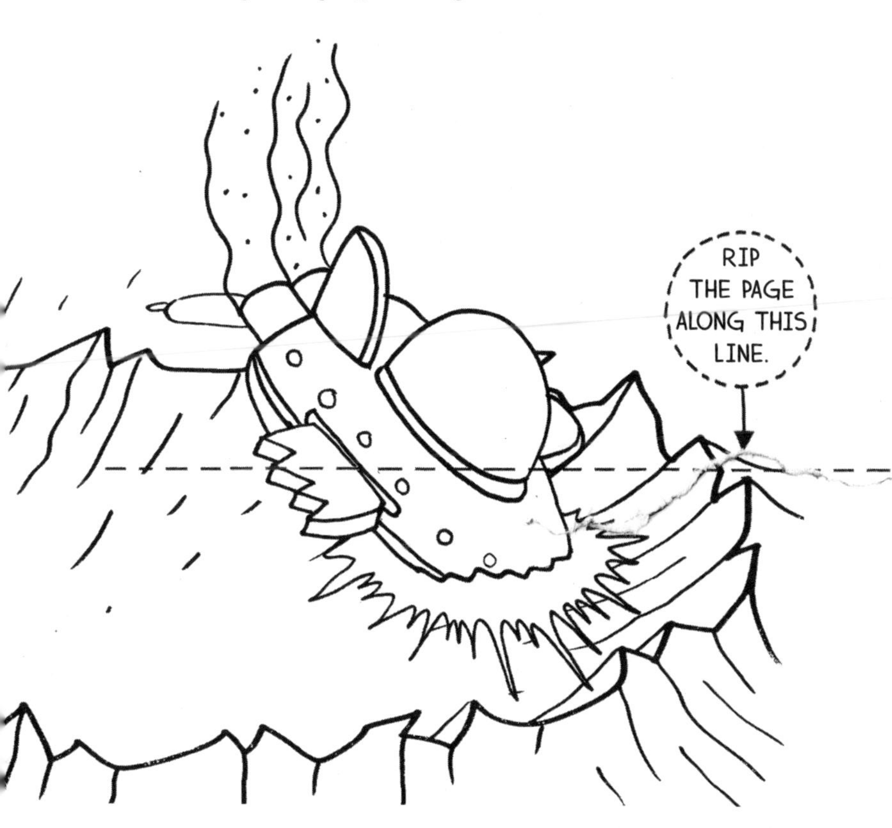

Daisy decides to peep inside. Maybe the alien is hiding in there. Would you be brave enough to do that?

I wouldn't. **NO WAY!**

Daisy peers inside the damaged spaceship. It is very dark and she can't see much.

If only I had a flashlight, she thinks.

There's a good idea. Draw her a flashlight so she can see inside.

CLICK!

The flashlight turns on and...

"AAAAAH!"

screams Daisy.

DRAW AN ALIEN HERE.

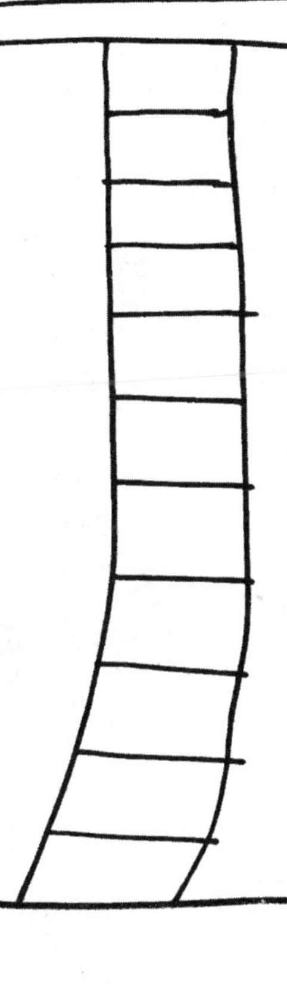

"7777774!"

screams the alien.

"Excuse me," says Daisy, "but what did you say?"

"[illegible]," says the alien.

"That's what I thought," says Daisy, stroking her chin and looking thoughtful.

The alien looks at her with big sad eyes (three of them). Can you Hear me

"[illegible]?" it says.

"We need to figure out a way to understand each other," says Daisy.

The alien pulls a strange device out of its pocket. I know. It's not even wearing any clothes. Weird, huh? It hands Daisy the device, which has "**TRANSLATOR**" written on it.

I bet you are thinking "Could this be an alien language translator?"

Yes. Yes, it is. Well done.

This is how it works. You fill in all the letters of the alphabet, and Daisy will be able to translate the alien language. Cool, huh?

Good job! Now let's see if the translator is working.

"[illegible]?" says the alien.

Daisy presses the ON button.

BLIP!

"Can you understand me?" says the alien.

Wow! It works! Isn't technology **GREAT**!?

The alien is **SO EXCITED** that he bursts into tears and starts talking without taking a breath.

"MY NAME IS B'OBSTRRRRK(FLN)TP AND I'M HUNGRY AND I'M LOST AND I DON'T KNOW WHERE I AM AND I'M HUNGRY AND I WANT TO GO HOME AND I'M HUNGRY AND I NEED HELP!"

(Big breath!)

"AND I'M HUNGRY," he says finally.

"It's okay, B'obstrrrk(fln)tp, I'll help you," says Daisy. "But do you mind if I call you B'ob?"

B'ob is delighted. "Not at all," he says. "What's your name?"

"It's Daisy," says Daisy.

"What a weird name," says B'ob. "But I like it."

Poor B'ob is hungry. Did he mention that?

"First things first," says Daisy. "Let's get you something to eat."

What do you think an alien would like to eat?

Oh yeah?

Let's draw it for him then.

Now that B'ob has eaten your delicious pizza/ hot dogs/carrots/chocolate cake (or whatever you drew) he is feeling much better.

"Okay," says Daisy. "Time to fix this spaceship."

They are going to need some tools. You can help by drawing some.

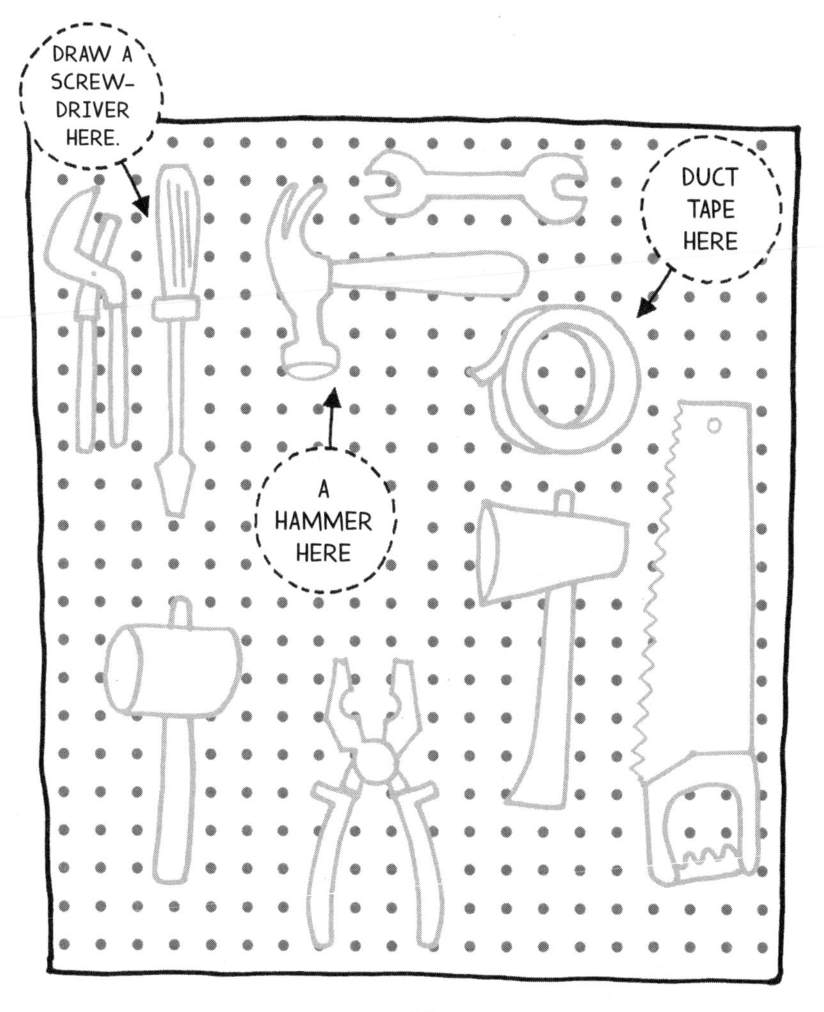

There was a lot of damage in the crash. Daisy figures out that they need to reconnect the equipment and make sure everything is working first.

Draw some wires to join up the connectors. Different colors would help. Just make sure **THE WIRES DO NOT CROSS.**

Connect the two **RED** wires.

Connect the two **BLUE** wires.

Connect the two **YELLOW** wires.

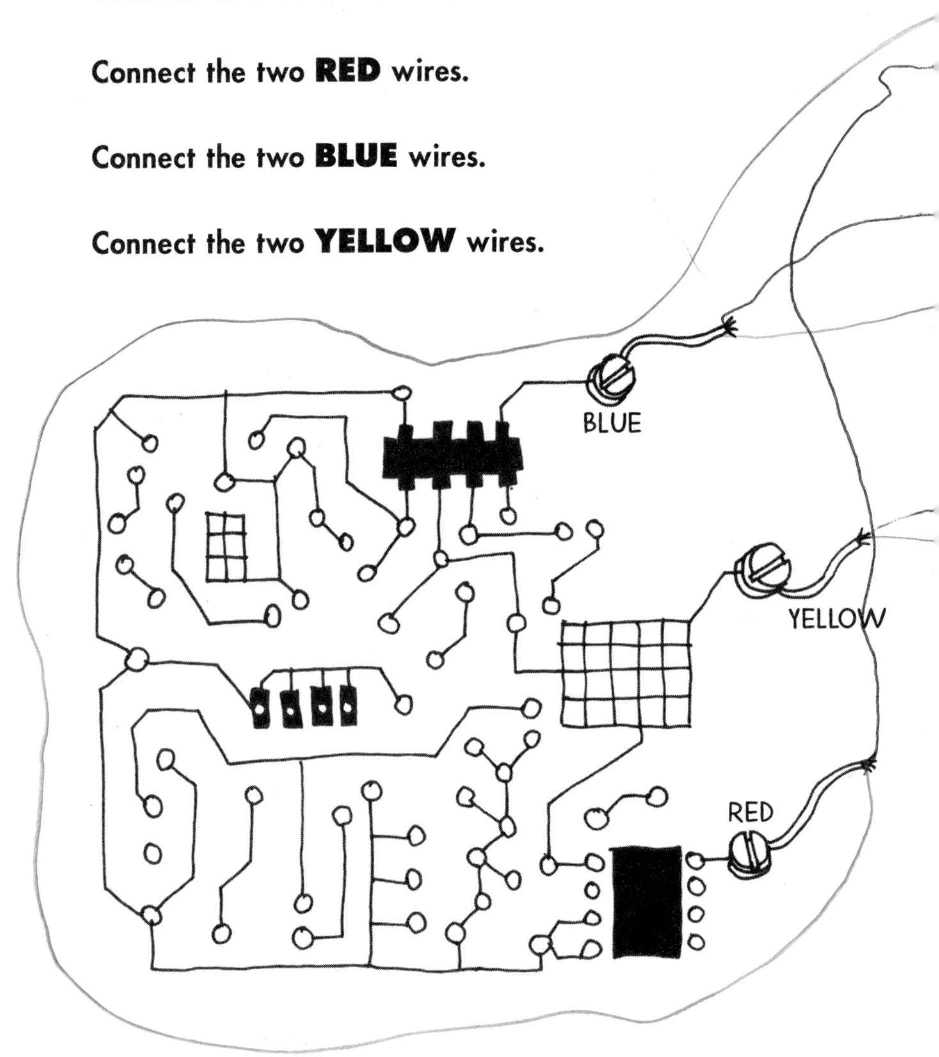

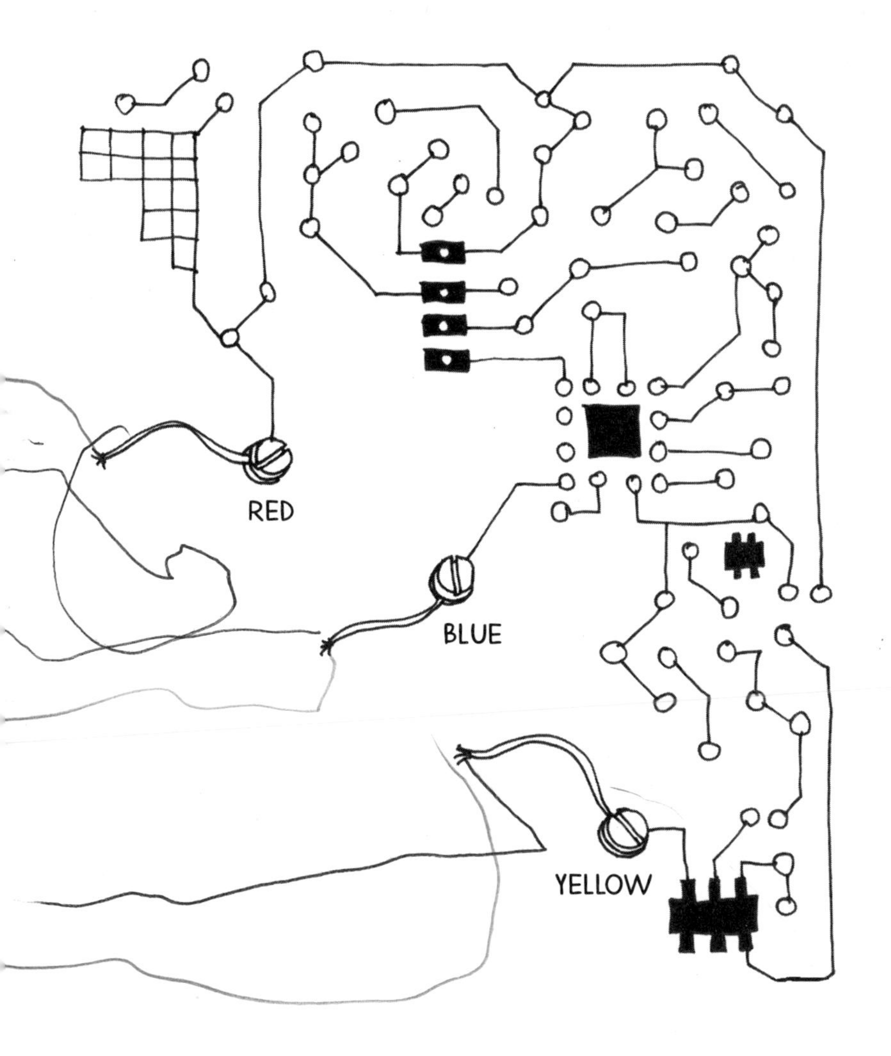

When the rewiring is finished, Daisy checks it carefully. "It looks good! Let's hope it works."

The ship is nearly ready for takeoff. Only one more thing needs to be done.

"We need to fix the broken wings," says Daisy. "Do you have any tape?"

If you do, then go back to page 43 and tape the page. But don't worry if you don't have any tape. Just keep the pages closed very tightly when the spaceship takes off.

We're ready to start the neutron engine. How fast can you draw a spiral? Faster than the speed of light, I hope, because you need to get this engine spinning!

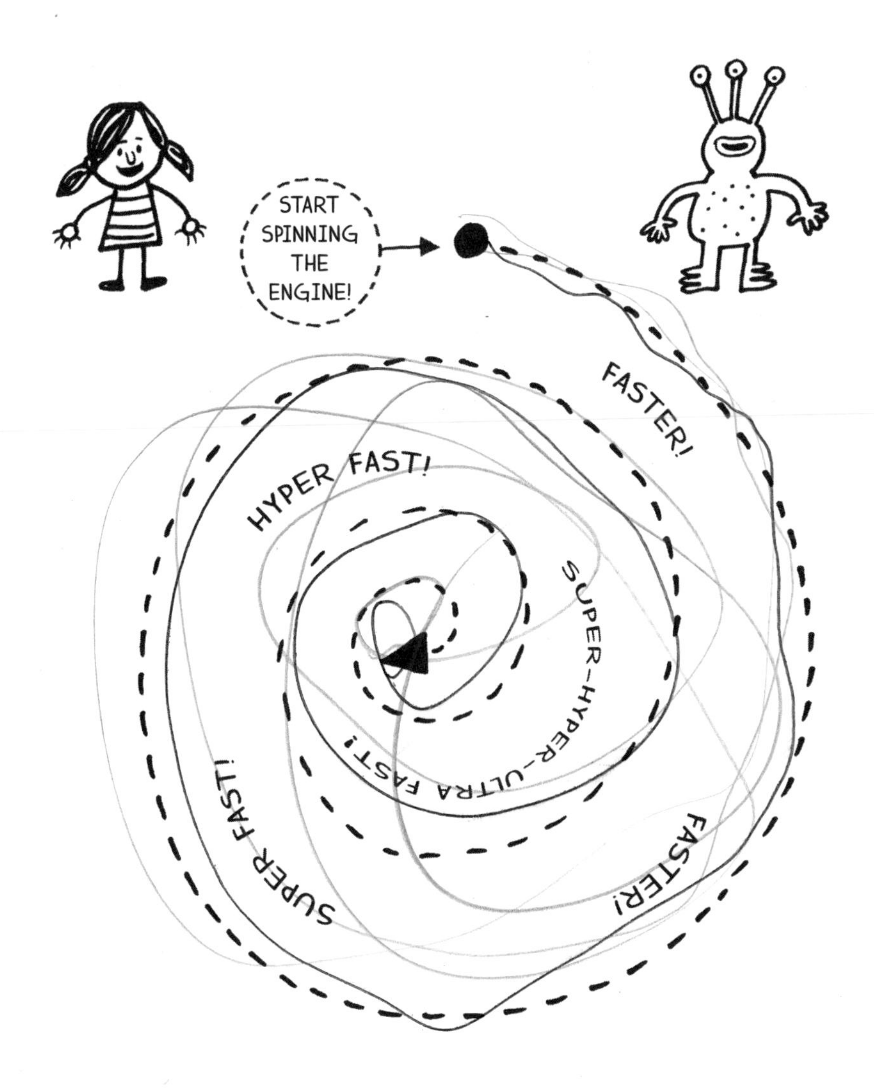

Wow! You sure are fast on the draw! The engine is spinning **SUPER-HYPER-ULTRA FAST**!

"Cool," says Daisy, watching as the engine glows brighter and brighter.

"**WHOOSH**," says the engine with a sudden flash.

B'ob points excitedly. "Look at that! We just made a spinning pulsar star."

The engine is powered up. We're ready to **ROCK**!
Are you ready to press the LAUNCH button?

5...

4...

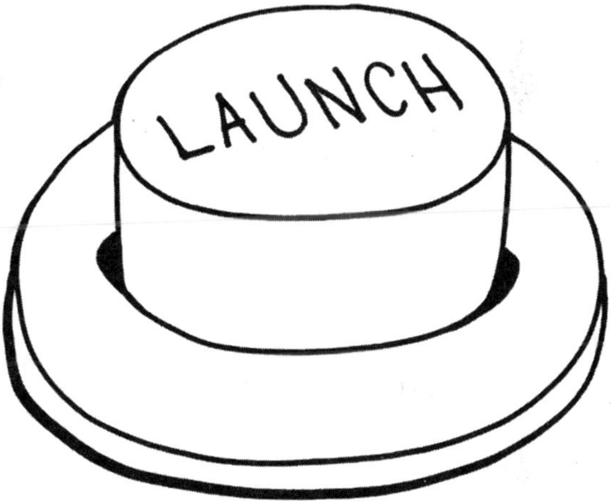

3...

2...

1... GO!

The whole spaceship rattles and shakes as the engines roar. The ship prepares for launch. Daisy and B'ob are holding on as tightly as they can to their seats.

"**WAHOOO!**" says B'ob.

Suddenly Daisy realizes they forgot to fix the steering wheel. "Oh no! There's no way to steer this thing!"

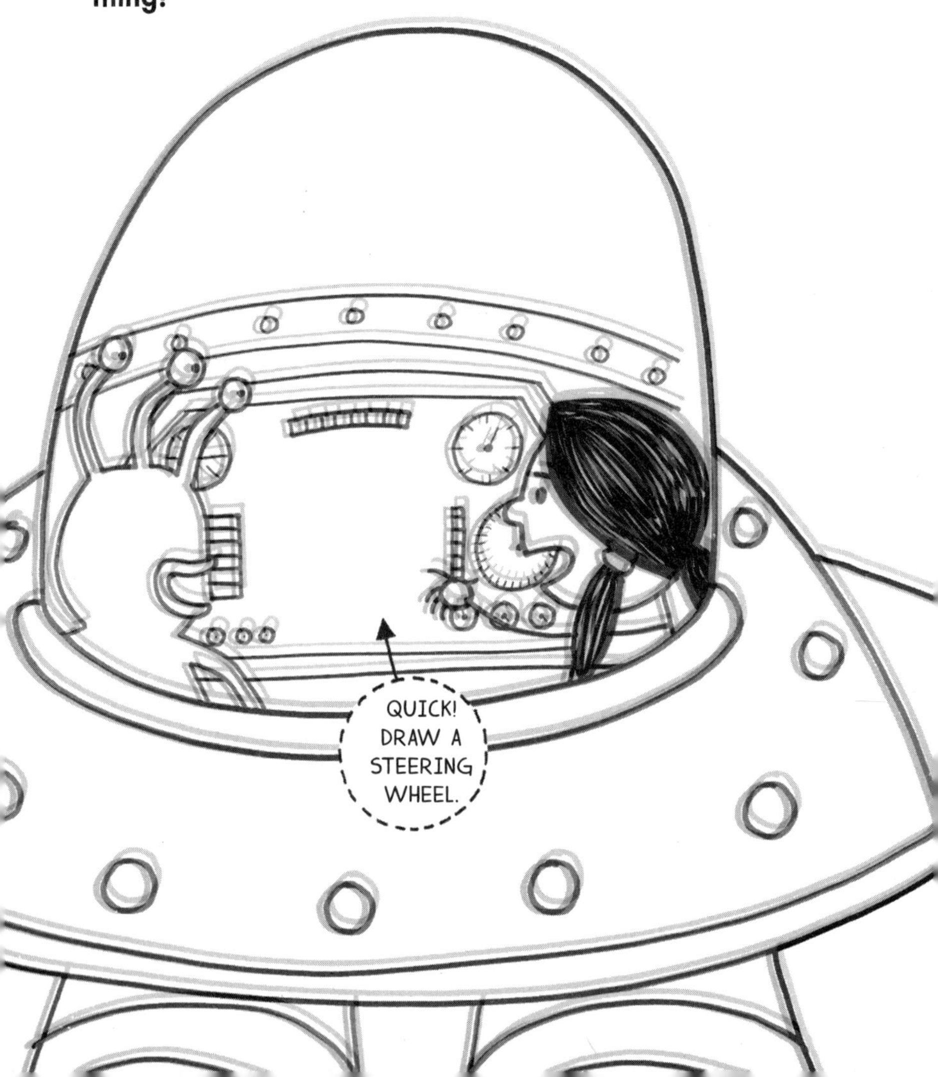

The spaceship **LEAPS** off the ground and rockets skyward, leaving a huge trail of smoke.

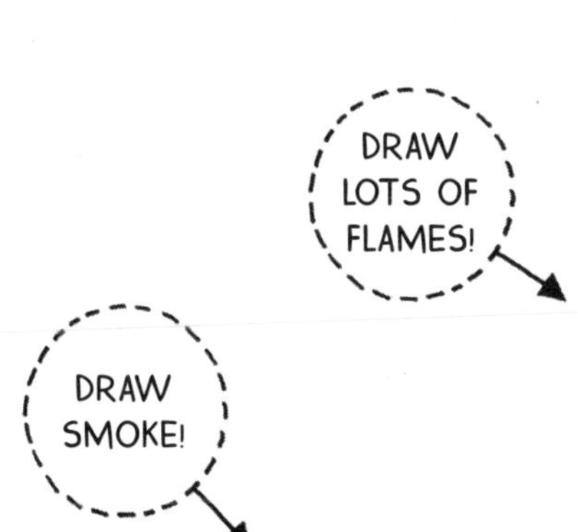

CHAPTER FOUR
SPACE!

The spaceship **SHOOTS** into orbit.

"This is cool," says Daisy. "Where to next?"

"Home," says B'ob as he sets the GPS. "If you'd like to visit?"

The ship accelerates away from Planet Scratchpad and out into space. Daisy and B'ob look out the window. There goes the moon!

"I thought there would be more craters," says Daisy.

She's right. It looks very blank. Draw in some craters.

The GPS flashes a warning as they enter an asteroid field.

"Hang on," says B'ob, holding the steering wheel tightly. "This could be rough."

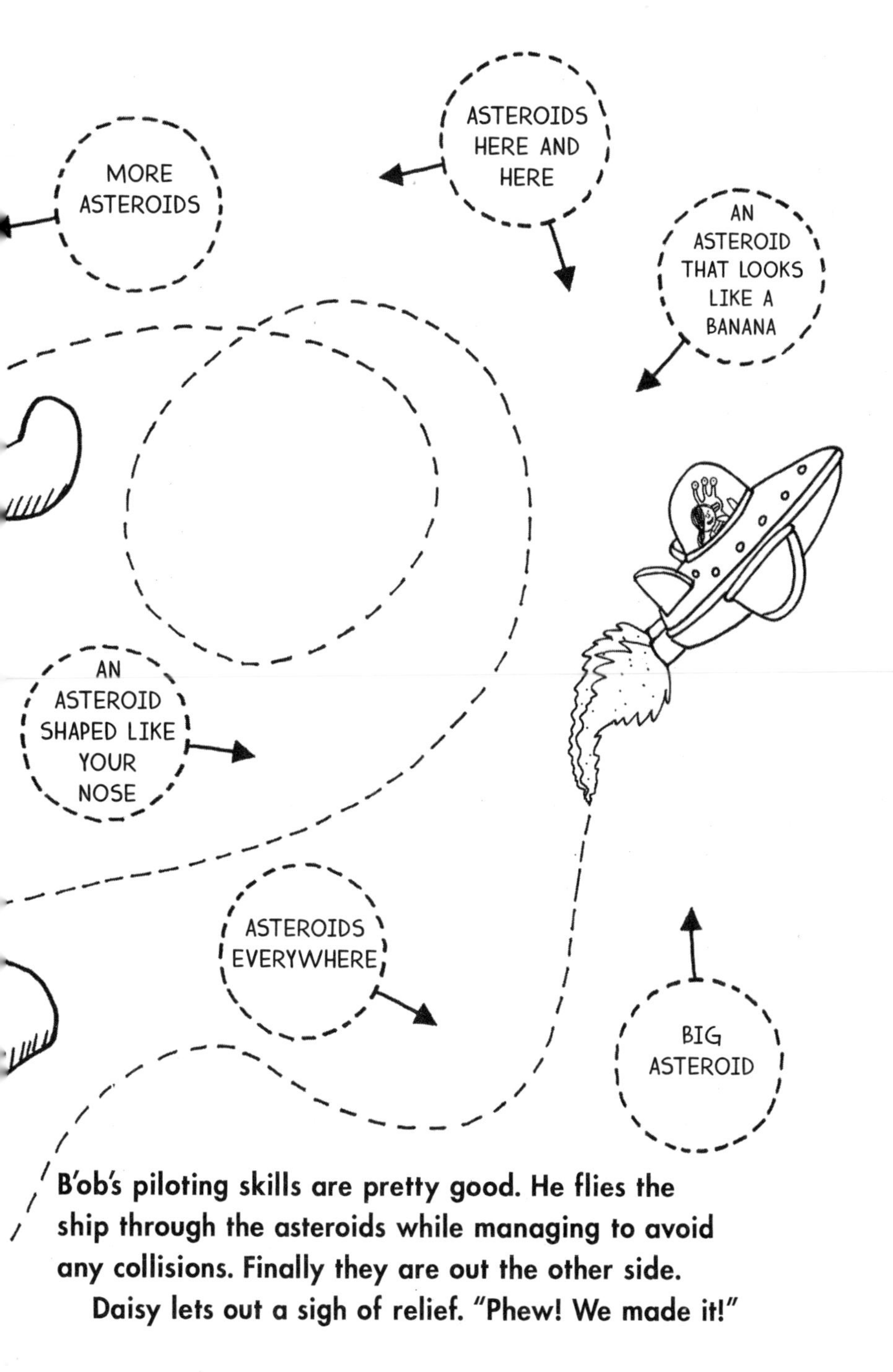

B'ob's piloting skills are pretty good. He flies the ship through the asteroids while managing to avoid any collisions. Finally they are out the other side.

Daisy lets out a sigh of relief. "Phew! We made it!"

B'ob and Daisy catch their breath while they study the star map.

"How do you plan to get home?" Daisy asks B'ob. "It looks like a long way."

B'ob gives her a wink with two of his eyes. "That's easy! We use the warp engine to fold space!"

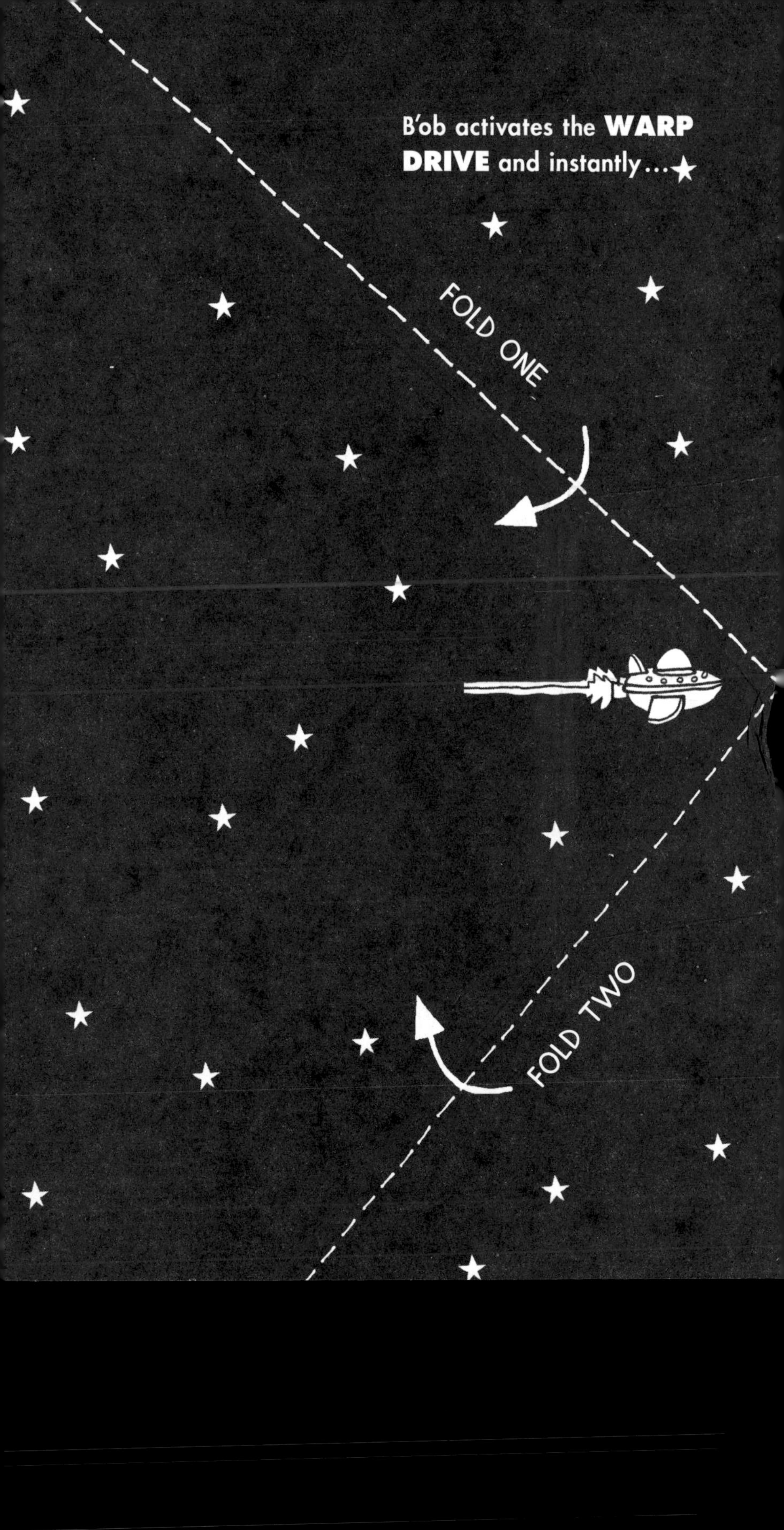
B'ob activates the **WARP DRIVE** and instantly...
FOLD ONE
FOLD TWO

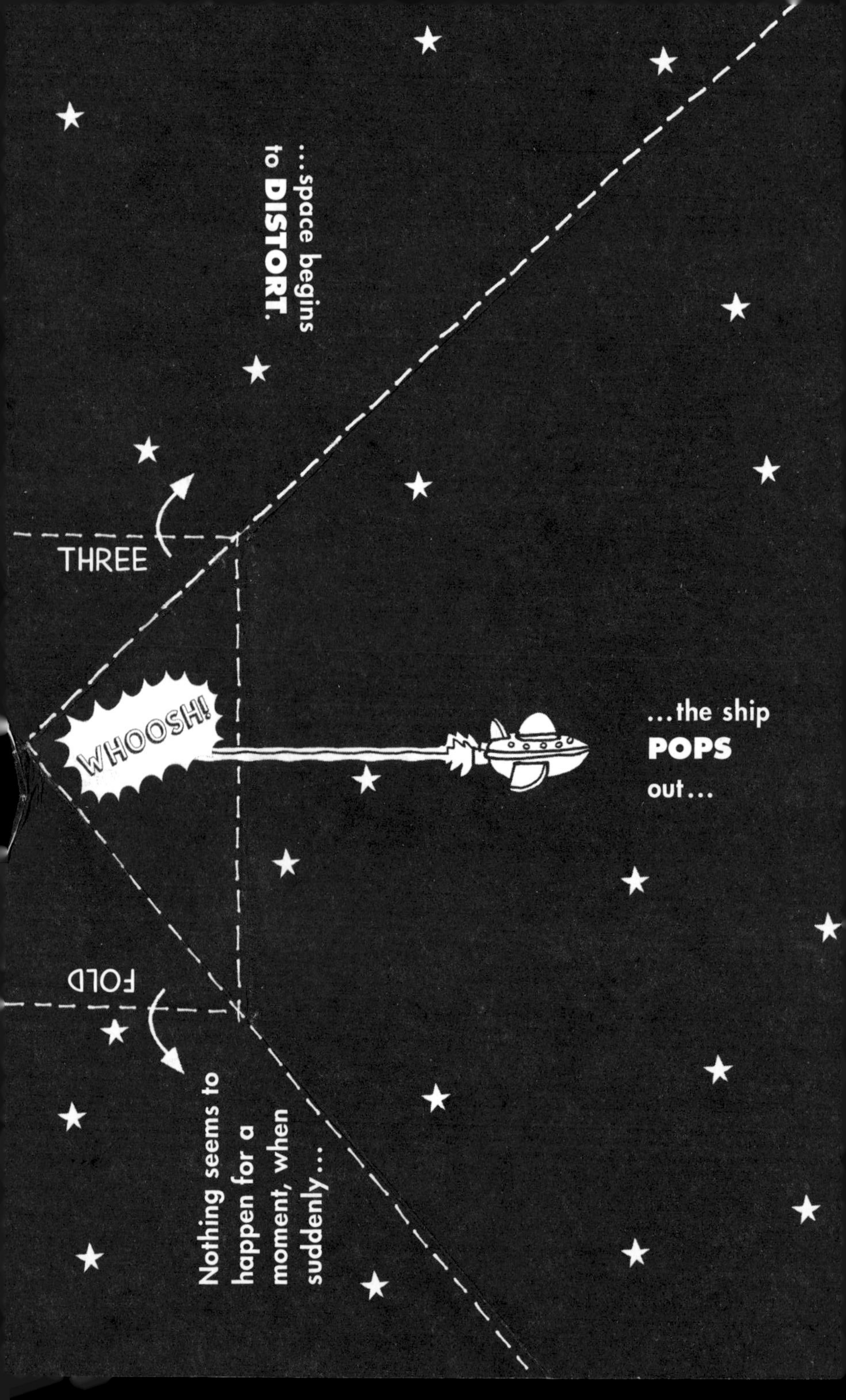

Nothing seems to happen for a moment, when suddenly...
...space begins to **DISTORT**.
THREE
FOLD
WHOOSH!
...the ship **POPS** out...

...on the **OTHER SIDE** of the galaxy!

CHAPTER FIVE

TROUBLE!

The spaceship enters orbit around Planet Grayscale just as the fuel warning light starts flashing.

B'ob looks nervous. "We've got to land this thing. We are way low on gas."

Daisy stares at the control panel. "Hmm. Which button should we press?"

Can you help? Choose a button to press.

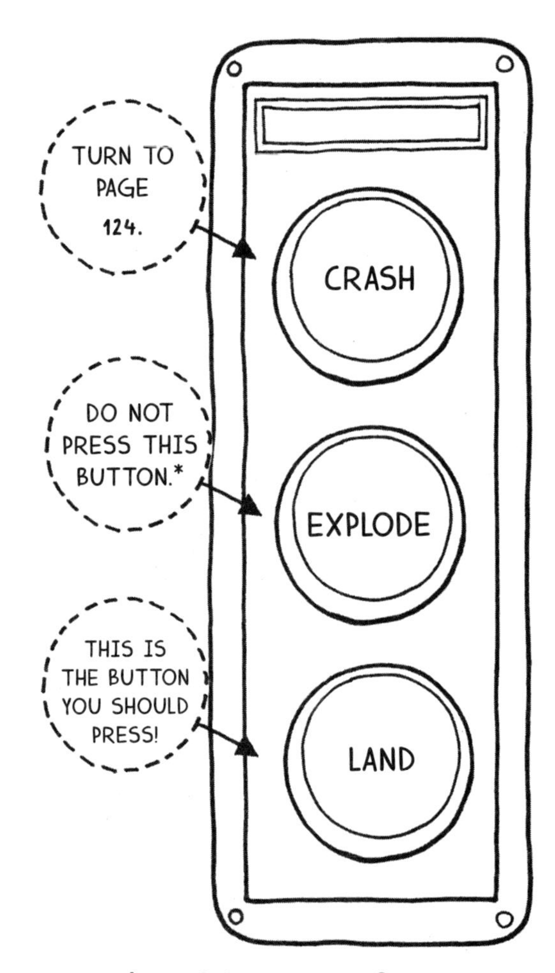

*What? You pressed the EXPLODE button? Are you crazy? Turn to page 125.

You pressed the LAND button. Good choice!

The autopilot takes over and guides the spaceship down toward the surface of the planet while Daisy looks out the window.

She notices something odd. "Everything is gray!"

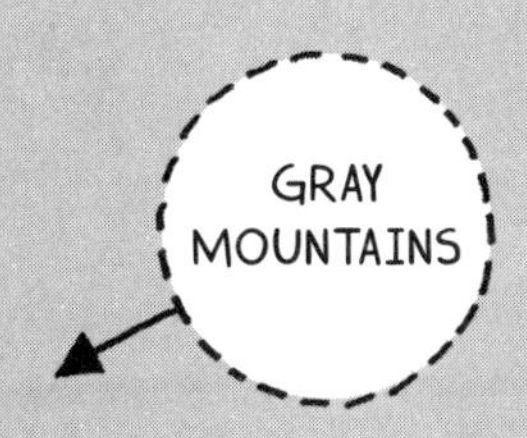

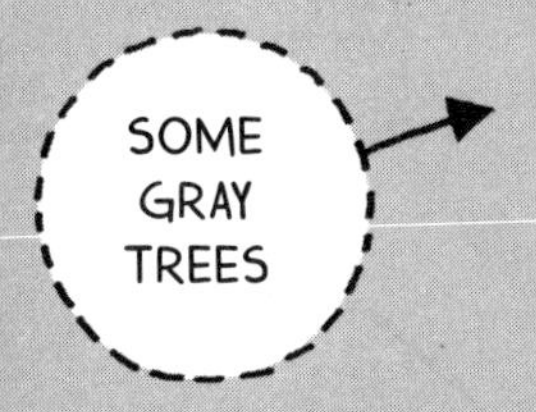

They fly over gray oceans, gray beaches, gray roads, and gray fields.

"Look! There's my house." B'ob points out the window.

The spaceship lands and B'ob opens the door. Just as Daisy is climbing out, a small alien runs out of the house.

"Uh-oh! It's my little sister," says B'ob from the corner of his mouth.

B'ob's sister marches up to him. "You are in **SO** much trouble!"

Suddenly an **ENORMOUS, SCARY** alien bursts from the house!

The monster roars with anger.

"B'OBSTRRRK(FLN)TP!!"

It lunges at B'ob and…

...picks him up to give him a **BIG HUG**.

"Thank goodness you are okay," it says. "Don't you ever take my spaceship again without permission."

B'ob looks embarrassed. "Sorry, Mom."

Daisy is invited to stay for dinner.

Unfortunately dinner doesn't look too appetizing. It's gray and dull.

Daisy pokes at the food on her plate. "I think this would look much tastier if it had some color."

Can you add some color to the food on the table?

B'ob's mom is impressed by your work. "Oh my! These colors are lovely. I had forgotten how much I love color."

She stares wistfully out the window.

"I remember a time when **EVERYTHING** was colorful. That was before the president took over and made everything gray."

Have you heard about the president before?

No?

You're lucky! Wait until you meet him...

"I wonder," says Mom to herself. "I think I may still have some old colorful things somewhere upstairs..."

Later that evening, when Daisy and B'ob have finished dinner (or at least tasted some of it out of **GOOD MANNERS**), they decide to go exploring.

"Can I bring Daisy into town?" B'ob asks his mom. She looks sternly at both of them. "Well, all right. But be home by twenty o'clock."

B'ob and Daisy go out to **EXPLORE** the town. Everything is unfinished, just like at home in Doodletown.

Except it's worse than that.

It's **GRAY** and **BORING**!

Even the weird fruit on the tree is gray.

They walk farther into town, where things get even grayer. Daisy begins to feel sorry for everyone. "They all look so unhappy."

"You're right." B'ob looks around thoughtfully. "I never really noticed before."

As Daisy and B'ob walk through town they notice posters on every wall.

STAY GRAY

BY ORDER OF THE PRESIDENT

NO COLOR.
NO PROBLEM.

BY ORDER OF THE PRESIDENT

COLOR?
WHO
CARES!

BY ORDER OF THE PRESIDENT

Daisy points to one of the posters. "Who is that guy?"

"That's the president," says B'ob. "He's the one who banned all color around here."

Daisy gives B'ob a big grin. "Well, maybe we should color **HIM** then."

Do you want to try?
Go on, I **DARE** you! Color the poster in!

Have you finished coloring in the poster?

☐ NO? Hurry up! We need to get on with the story.

☐ YES? Excellent! Let's continue.

The poster looks great now. Good job! Daisy and B'ob step back to admire your handiwork. They do not notice someone standing right beside them.

UH-OH! It's the **SHERIFF**. And he does **NOT** look impressed!

Daisy and B'ob jump as he lets out a roar. "**WHAT'S GOING ON HERE? DID YOU DRAW ON THAT POSTER?**"

The sheriff is really annoyed. "Who gave you permission to be here?"

Daisy does some fast thinking. She remembers the **PERMISSION SLIP** you tore out of the book earlier! Do you still have it? Go and get it so that Daisy can show it to the sheriff.

Daisy hands the permission slip to the sheriff. He stares at it closely. He stares at Daisy. He stares back at the slip in confusion.

"What is this?" he asks. "Where are you from? Are you an alien?"

Before Daisy can answer, the sheriff makes his decision. "You are both in **BIG TROUBLE**. I'm taking you to see the president."

The sheriff takes Daisy and B'ob to the president's office. Guess who they meet there?

That's right, the president. Surprised? Well, you shouldn't be, because I told you he would be appearing soon.

He looks very annoyed. "Who are you? And why were you drawing on my lovely posters?" He glares at them both over his big show-off desk.

Look at him. He thinks he is so great.

Daisy is **NOT** impressed by him one little bit. She doesn't like being bossed around. "I'm Daisy. I'm from a planet where we draw on everything."

The president is not happy with her answer. "Is that so? And you think that gives you the right to color my poster?"

Daisy looks the president straight in the eye. "I thought it needed some cheering up."

The president thumps the desk. "Nonsense!" he says. "We like things the way they are. One shade of gray is exciting enough for us, thank you very much."

The president drones on and on about color and gray and blah and blah.

Daisy's mind begins to wander. This guy is **SO** boring, she thinks.

She's right. He doesn't even **LOOK** like a president! Let's turn the page and do something about that.

Do your best to make him look **RIDICULOUS**! Draw a silly-looking **CROWN** and some crazy **EYELASHES**. What about a huge **MUSTACHE** or some lovely red **LIPSTICK**?

ANYTHING that makes him look funny!

Well done! The president looks really silly now. And **REALLY** annoyed. He screams and shouts and says things like:

"OUTRAGEOUS!"

and

"HOW DARE YOU!"

What a doofus.

Daisy, B'ob, and the sheriff can't help but laugh.

The president roars at the sheriff, "Take them away! Lock them in the zoo!"

The sheriff tries to stop snickering as he marches them away. He puts them in a van and locks the door.

This doesn't look too good...

CHAPTER SIX

ZOO!

Daisy and B'ob arrive at the zoo, which is where the aliens go on Sundays to stare at weird-looking creatures, like **DAISY**!

Remember: If you visited Planet Grayscale, you would be the weird-looking alien, too!

The sheriff marches them through the entrance.

They pass a cage with a **BLORTHAK TROON** in it. As I'm sure you know, a blorthak troon is a large, monstrous creature with **TEN ARMS**. It is very hairy and scary, with a mouth full of sharp teeth, but it is in fact quite cuddly and has a lovely smile.

Do your best drawing of a blorthak troon in the cage.

Daisy is impressed with the blorthak troon. "Whoa! She would be a good goalkeeper for our soccer team."

Daisy and B'ob are locked in enclosures next to two other creatures.

The first is a **WINDLE**, which is a large blob with four eyes, two wobbly ears, and a nice haircut. It has a trunk that it uses to suck up small insects.

The second is a **PLOMP**, a tiny creature the size of a dot. It is so tiny that you can barely see its **FORTY LEGS** and **FORTY ARMS**. It also likes to wear tiny hats.

Daisy is feeling very sorry for herself. "What are we going to do, B'ob? This adventure isn't going so well."

B'ob has no answer. He is too busy worrying what his mom will say when she finds out he has been put in the zoo.

What would your mother say if you were locked in a zoo?

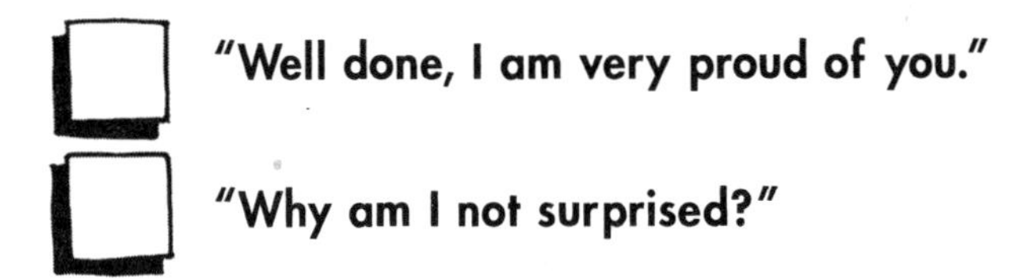

"Well done, I am very proud of you."

"Why am I not surprised?"

I bet you are thinking things can't get much worse.

WRONG!

Because here comes...

...the president.

He is very smug and full of himself. "You are not so clever now, eh, Doodle?"

"I didn't mean any harm," says Daisy.

"That's not good enough," says the president. "I'm going to teach you a lesson."

What a meanie.

He shows Daisy his plan. She studies it, becoming more and more horrified.

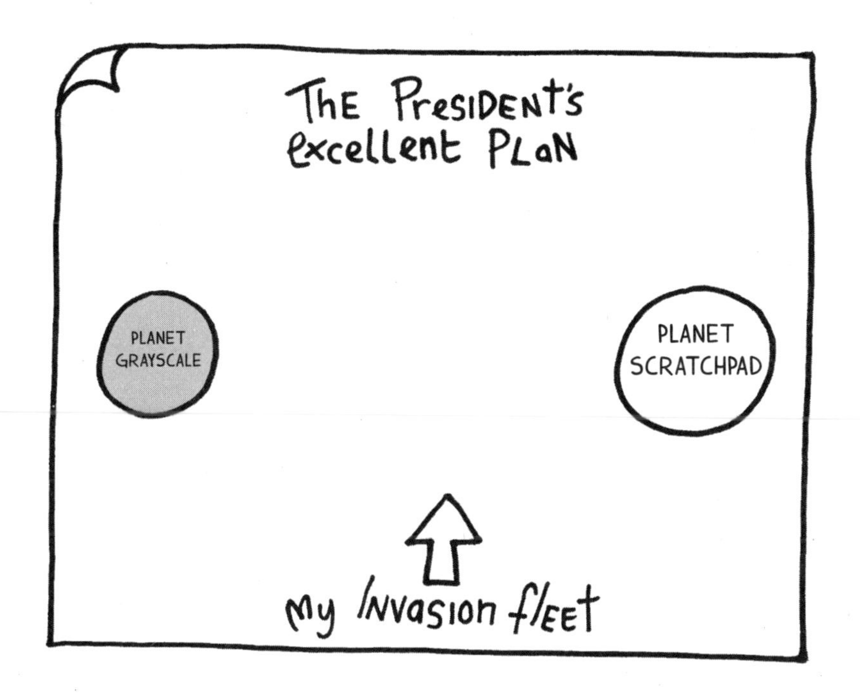

The president is delighted with himself. "I am going to invade your home planet with my fleet of five hundred seventy-three spaceships* and make everything **GRAY**!"

OH NO!

*What do you mean you can't see 573 spaceships? You're supposed to draw them!

CHAPTER SEVEN

ESCAPE!

After the president has gone, Daisy sits down to think. This is **PRETTY BAD**! What is she going to do?

Just then a voice says, "I could help if you want."

Daisy spins around. "Undrawn John! Where did you come from?"

"I've been with you all this time," says John. "I just wasn't drawn."

Well! Isn't **THAT** a nice surprise? John deserves to be **DRAWN** for that, don't you think?

Undrawn John has a plan. He reaches into his pocket and takes out...

HIS INVISIBLE PENCIL!

Have you ever seen an invisible pencil? No? Me neither. John holds up his invisible pencil (at least, Daisy thinks he does).

"It's not very good for drawing," he says, "but it's great for undrawing."

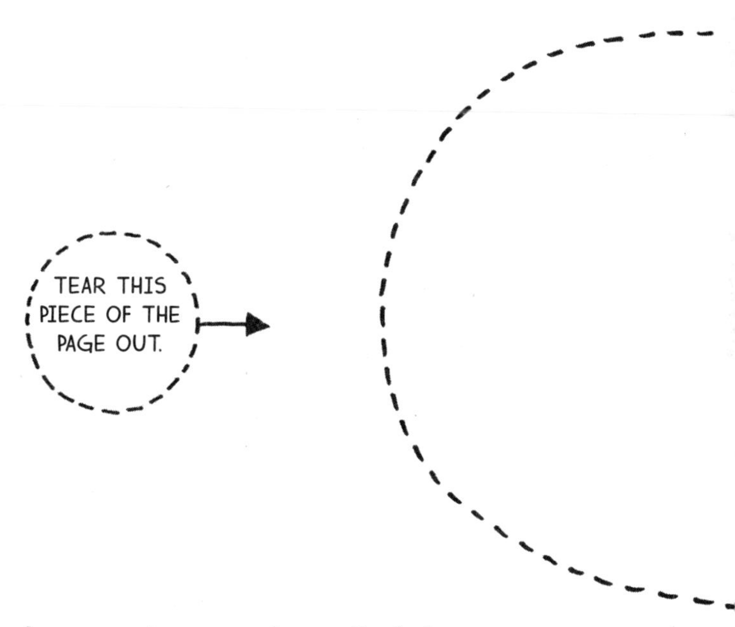

Carefully he draws a shape on the wall of the cage.

Daisy watches in **AMAZEMENT** as the side of the cage **DISAPPEARS**. "Wow! I can't believe what I'm not seeing."

Daisy and Undrawn John jump from the cage and run to free B'ob.

But they are quickly spotted by the sheriff and the zoo attendant. Time to get out of here!

They run through the zoo looking for a way to **ESCAPE**.

Which way should they go?

☐ To the exit door? Turn to page 96.

☐ To the big balloon in the sky? Turn to page 100.

So you decided to escape through the **EXIT** door?

The **EXIT** leads to a small room with a platform and a control panel. It's a **TELEPORTER**!

"Great! We can teleport out of here," says B'ob.

There are **THREE** buttons. Which will you press?

Whoops! It looks like you pressed the wrong button. You've **SWAPPED** everybody's heads!

"What the..." says Daisy/B'ob/Undrawn John.

You had better try again.

Oh dear. You are not very good at working a teleporter, are you?

Daisy looks down. "Where's the rest of me?"

"Urg! My head is where my feet should be," says Undrawn John.

Try again!

FINALLY, you press the correct button. The teleporter works properly.

"At last," says Daisy. "Let's get out of here."

Now turn to page 104.

Daisy, B'ob, and Undrawn John run to the balloon and grab hold just as it TAKES OFF.

But it isn't a **BALLOON**! It's a

GASEOUS SPRONG!

Daisy, B'ob, and Undrawn John cling on tightly as they float higher and higher.

The **GASEOUS SPRONG** releases some stinky gas!

It is **SO STINKY** that they all let go of the gaseous sprong.

Guess what happens? You got it! They start falling.

Quickly! Draw something soft for them to land on.

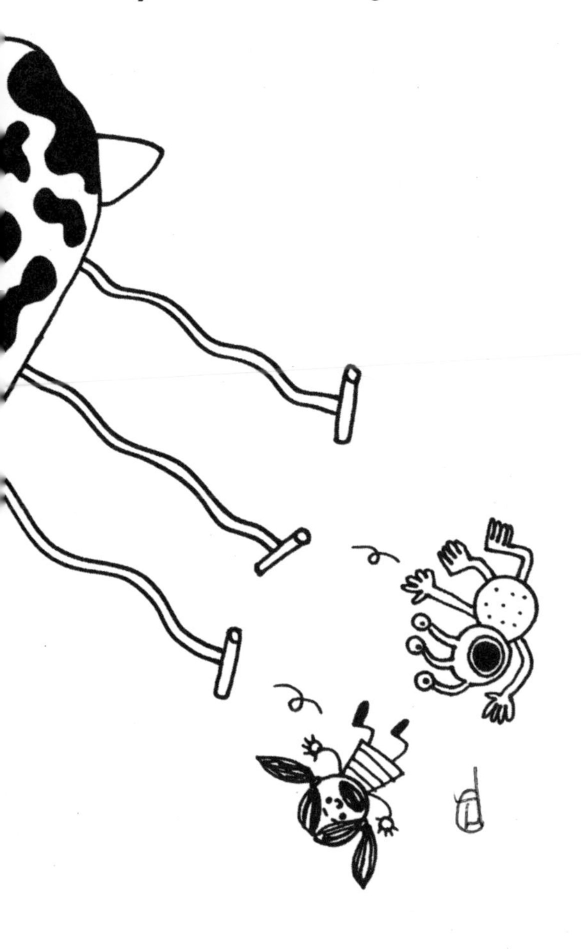

At last Daisy, B'ob, and Undrawn John have escaped the zoo.

Daisy looks around desperately. "We need to find somewhere to hide."

"Follow me," says B'ob. "I know just the place."

They all run down the street with B'ob leading the way. Suddenly Daisy stops and points to the sky. "Oh no! Look!"

The sky is filled with spaceships! The president's **INVASION FLEET** is launching.

DRAW A SPACESHIP.

They all stop and stare at the sky in horror.

"What are we going to do?" asks B'ob.

Undrawn John appears to be deep in thought. Or probably would if we could see him. Then he has a **BRILLIANT IDEA**!

"We are going to draw a super-fast spaceship, that's what!"

Draw a **SUPER-FAST** spaceship with some **COOL FINS**, a powerful **ENGINE**, and some nice **WING MIRRORS**.

Don't forget to add a **DOOR HANDLE**.

CHAPTER EIGHT

EPIC SPACE BATTLE!

With their new **AWESOME** spaceship, our heroes take off in hot pursuit. Soon they are closing in on the invasion fleet.

"Okay," says B'ob. "What's next?"

Guess who has just had **ANOTHER** brilliant idea? Undrawn John of course! He turns to Daisy and B'ob with a big grin. "What's the one thing the president hates the most?"

Of course! "**COLOR!**"

THIS ONE IS ORANGE!
GREEN!
GAK! GREEN!
NOT ORANGE! I HATE ORANGE!
OOH! PURPLE! I LIKE PURPLE!
PURPLE!
FASTER! COLOR THEM ALL!
RED!
BLUE!

The president is **NOT** impressed. "You've **RUINED** my invasion fleet!"

Look at him. He is having a tantrum, banging his fists on the dashboard. What a big baby.

"I'll get you!" he screams as he starts chasing Daisy and her friends.

He chases them all over space...

...until eventually he catches up with them. He squeals with delight. "I have you now!"

But then, just when things look **REALLY BAD**,
a voice shouts over the radio,

"LEAVE THOSE KIDS ALONE!"

Another spaceship drops out of the sky. Look who it is! It's B'ob's mom!

The president looks over his shoulder in horror. He is in **BIG TROUBLE** and he knows it.

He holds his breath as Mom takes aim.

ZAPPEW!

B'ob's mom zaps the president's spaceship with tons of **BRIGHT COLORS**. And we all know how much he hates bright colors.

COLOR THE PAGE!

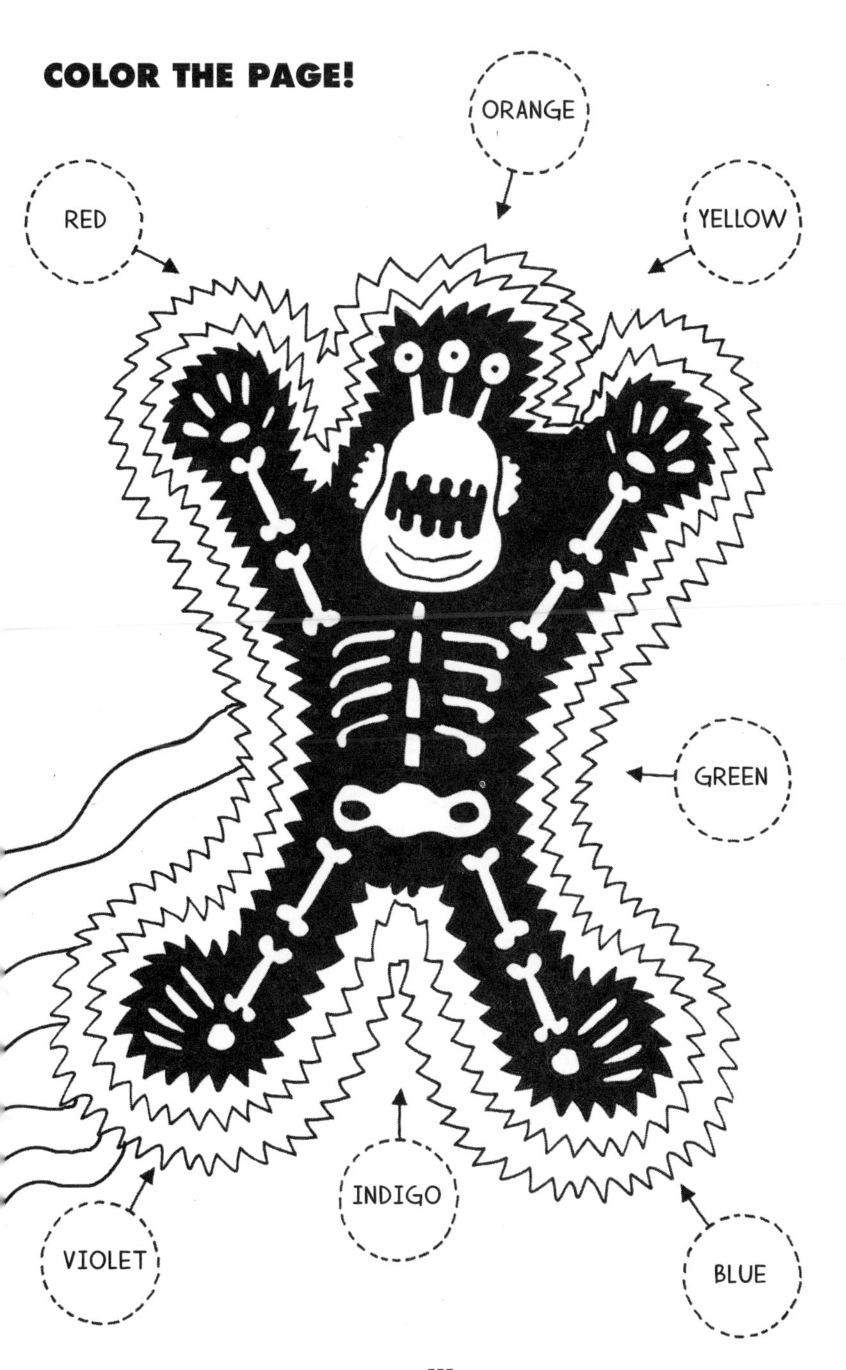

How awesome is B'ob's mom? How awesome are **ALL** moms?!

B'ob's mom chases the president right out of the book and then returns to land her spaceship.

A **BIG** crowd has gathered to watch the space battle. And they are all **CHEERING**!

Mom lands to a **HERO'S WELCOME**.

As she gets out of her spaceship, the crowd lifts her up and carries her on their shoulders. They all cheer and wave. They haven't been this happy in a long time.

CHAPTER NINE

MEDALS!

The people of Planet Grayscale decide to award Daisy, Undrawn John, and B'ob with

MEDALS!

What do you think the medals should look like?
Oh yeah? That sounds good. Draw the medal.

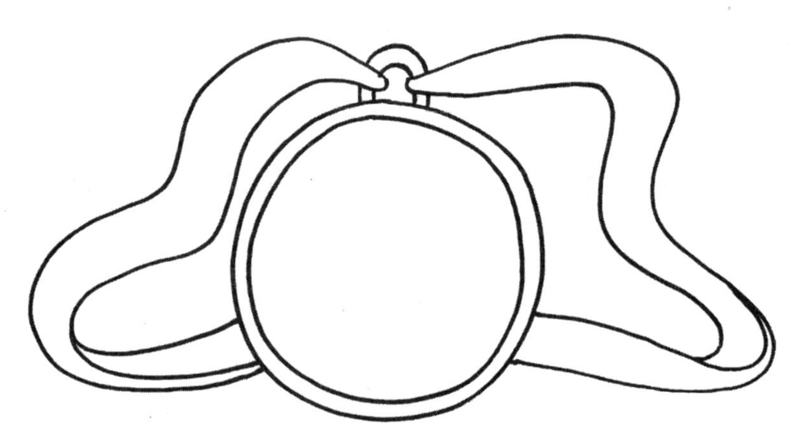

There is a **BIG PARTY** to celebrate. Our heroes line up to get their reward.

Can you draw the medals around their necks?

Well done! Everyone on Planet Grayscale is delighted, especially the new president...

MOM!

It is time for Daisy and Undrawn John to go home. They leave behind a very different world than the one they found when they arrived.

Planet Grayscale is going to have to change its name, I think. Can **YOU** think of an awesome new name?

And soon enough they are back at Planet Scratchpad. Daisy and Undrawn John look out the window at the beautiful world below them. They have never been so happy to see home.

Undrawn John points. "Look. I can see Smile Island."

DRAW SMILE ISLAND.

B'ob takes them in to land. Below them they can see their **SCHOOL**!

EVERYONE is waiting excitedly on the playground.

Miss Scribble is shocked to see Daisy climb out of a spaceship.

"Where have you been, Daisy Doodle?" she asks.

"You are not going to believe this, Miss Scribble," says Daisy.

Everybody listens in **AWE** as Daisy tells the story.

"But I couldn't have done it without the help of one special person," says Daisy. "He is the one person in our class that we should **ALL** pay more attention to."

She is talking, of course, about

UNDRAWN JOHN.

Everyone cheers for Undrawn John. Let's draw him a **HAT** so that everybody will know where he is from now on.

Now there is only one thing left to do...

Let's give B'ob a **BIG SENDOFF**!

THE END

What? You want more?

Okay. Go back to the start and...

COLOR IT ALL IN!

Oh dear. You **CRASHED** the spaceship! Well, at least everyone is safe.

Turn to page 72.

THE END

Well, that was silly. Go back to page 68 and try again.

Remember: **DO NOT PRESS EXPLODE!**

How to Draw B'ob:

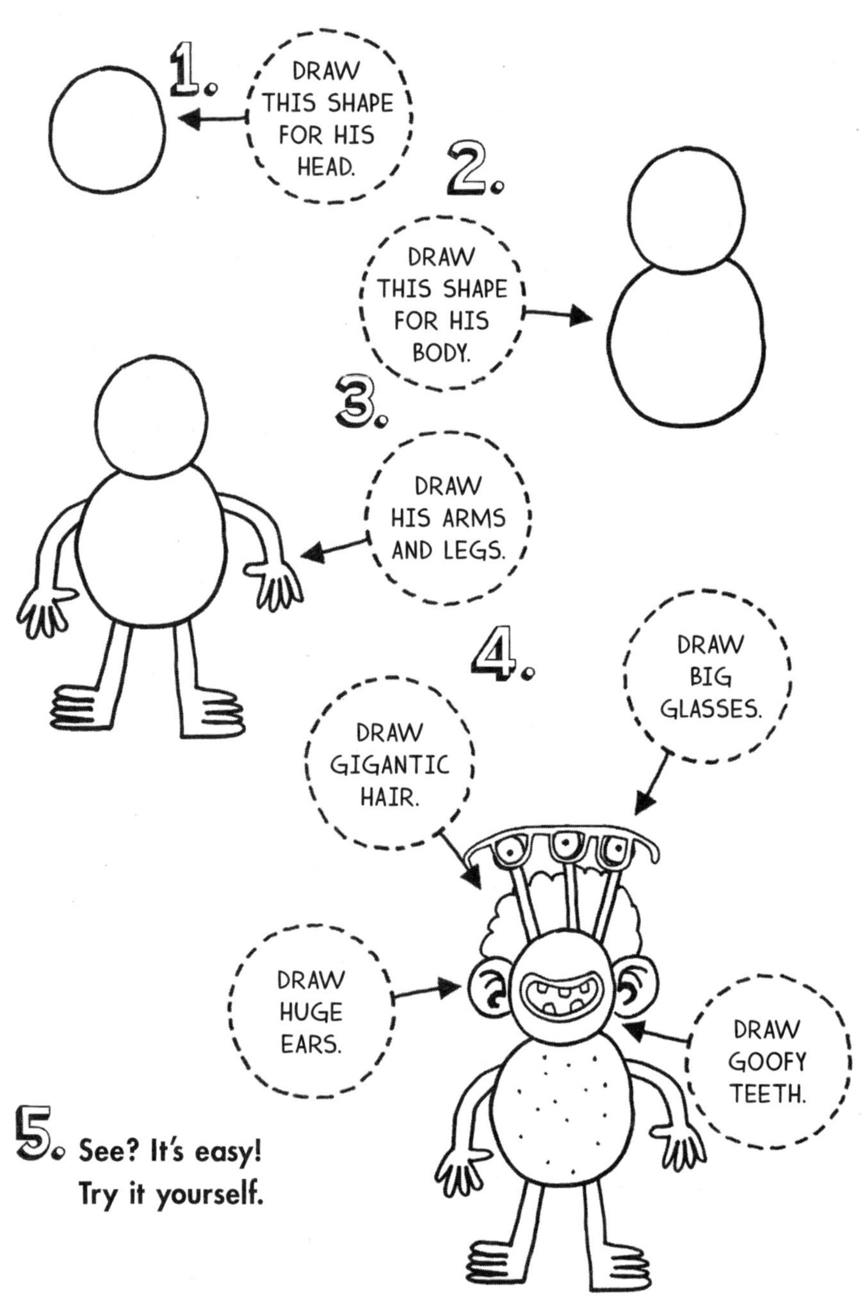

PERMISSION SLIP

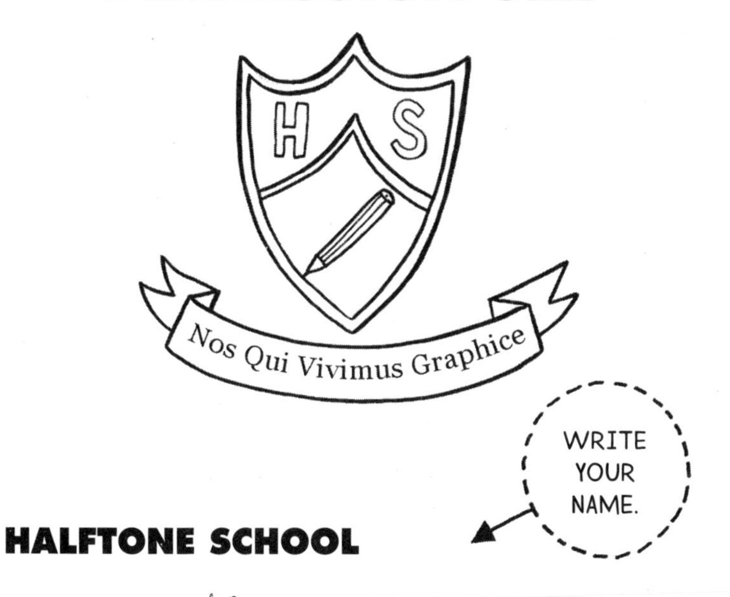

WRITE YOUR NAME.

HALFTONE SCHOOL

Daisy and ____Undrawn Jhon____ are hereby given permission to leave the school grounds to chase an alien.

Signed: Principal Rule

P.S. Make sure you are back by the end of the day.

Tear out this slip and remember to **KEEP IT WITH YOU** at all times. Now go back to the page you were on.

THE END*

Bye-bye!

*Just kidding! Go back to page 12.